Montague Chamberlain, Andreas T. Hagerup, Frimann B.
Arngrimson

The Birds of Greenland

Montague Chamberlain, Andreas T. Hagerup, Frimann B. Arngrimson

The Birds of Greenland

ISBN/EAN: 9783337316068

Printed in Europe, USA, Canada, Australia, Japan

Cover: Foto ©Andreas Hilbeck / pixelio.de

More available books at **www.hansebooks.com**

THE

BIRDS OF GREENLAND.

By ANDREAS T. HAGERUP.

Translated from the Danish

BY

FRIMANN B. ARNGRIMSON.

EDITED BY MONTAGUE CHAMBERLAIN.

BOSTON:
LITTLE, BROWN, AND COMPANY.
1891.

EDITOR'S PREFACE.

I HAVE little to say by way of preface, more than to thank Mr. Hagerup for permitting my name to be associated with the American edition of his work. My own labor upon it has been very light, — a few suggestions to author and translator, and a few notes.

M. CHAMBERLAIN.

Foxcroft House,
    Cambridge, Mass.

PREFACE.

THROUGH Mr. Chamberlain's kind assistance there was published in "The Auk," Vol. VI., Nos. 3 and 4, an article on the birds of Ivigtut, the result of my observations during fifteen months' residence at that place.

Since that article was written, I have spent another fifteen months in the same locality, and have been able to add considerably to my previous notes. It is partly because of this, and partly because a few errors crept into my former article, — errors due to my imperfect knowledge of English and to insufficient mail service between Greenland and the North American continent (only twice a year), — that I have expressed the wish to publish as complete a description of the birds of Ivigtut as my two and a half years' residence there enables me to write ; and with characteristic liberality Mr. Chamberlain has undertaken the entire responsibility of bringing out an American edition. At his request I have also .

compiled from published and unpublished documents, and other sources, a catalogue of the birds that have been observed in Greenland.

The nomenclature and classification I have followed is that adopted by the American Ornithologists' Union.

A: T. HAGERUP.

VIBORG, DENMARK.

INTRODUCTION.

THE mining town of Ivigtut is situated on the south side of Arsuk fjord in South Greenland (lat. 61° 15′, long. 48° 10′), and about ten miles distant from the open sea. This fjord is about twenty miles long by two in width, and is surrounded by cliffs rising one thousand to two thousand feet above the level of the sea, — one peak, Kunnak, reaching forty-four hundred feet. These cliffs are here and there broken by small valleys diversified by thick willow bushes and meadow plots, also by lakelets, and streams that teem with trout. On the uplands, among the hills, are several lakes of varying size; but there is very little vegetation, while the interior of the country is covered with eternal ice. A glacier extends down into Arsuk fjord and forms its inner terminus.

It is the fjord itself that at all seasons is the chief theatre of animal life. Polar bears, brought by the big ice, float in occasionally; whales, even three or four kinds, are frequent visitors; and seals, which form the principal food-supply of the Eskimos, are abundant. Close to where the ice descends into the fjord and the cliffs are steepest, a large number of Gulls hatch their eggs in summer, while during winter the open part of the fjord is visited by large flocks of Eider Ducks and Murres. Other swimmers do not enter so far into the fjord, but remain by the shore of the open sea, so that the Eskimos of Arsuk, which is about ten miles from Ivigtut, often brought a large number of birds which we, living inland, would not otherwise have seen.

The mean annual temperature is about 0° Cent., or a little less; and the whole country is usually covered with snow from the first of November to the first of May. The inner half of the fjord freezes over in November or the beginning of December, and is not free of ice till the end of May. At Ivigtut the ice leaves a month earlier. The willow bushes are out in leaf at the close of June, and the leaves fade from night frost about the 10th of September.

I remained at Ivigtut from April 22, 1886, to October 17, 1888.

BIRDS OF IVIGTUT.

LOON.

URINATOR IMBER.

QUITE common, as far as I have been able to learn. It does not arrive until the middle of May (earliest seen May 15), but remains through the whole season, and sometimes till late in the autumn. Thus I noticed one Nov. 18, 1887, the day before the fjord froze over. In the spring it is not seen on the fjord until the beginning of July, and hatches here very late, probably because the upland lakes are not yet free of ice. I have obtained from the Greenlanders several sets of eggs in July, and two sets taken in August.

RED-THROATED LOON.

URINATOR LUMME.

Common in the innermost part of the fjord during the whole summer. On the 21st of July, 1888, I 'found one pair with their young upon a small lake seven hundred feet above sea-level.

PUFFIN.

FRATERCULA ARCTICA.

An old bird was harpooned at Arsuk on the 15th of July, 1887.

BLACK GUILLEMOT.

CEPPHUS GRYLLE.

Very common throughout the year. Breeds in colonies of two to thirty pair among the precipitous cliffs along the fjord, during the middle and latter part of June. There is considerable variation in the time when the dif-. erent individuals moult. In April some have donned their summer garb, while others are still in their winter clothing. On the 13th of July I shot one which already had gray feathers among the black.

BRÜNNICH'S MURRE.

URIA LOMVIA.

A winter visitor,— the last seen May 30, 1886; the first returning seen Nov. 9, 1886, and on the next day they were common. During the following winter, which was very cold, these birds gathered by thousands on the fjord. On the 16th of April they were still numerous; but on the 25th of that month most of them had gone. Yet I saw on the 4th of June small groups of from two to five each, and on the 20th of June two single birds. In the winter of 1887–88, a comparatively mild winter, though the fjord remained almost completely covered with ice, I did not observe any of this species until the 27th of December, and then only a few single individuals, and these were often in company with Black Guillemots. During the entire winter there were only a few small flocks to be seen on the fjord, but large numbers were reported wintering at Arsuk. The last were observed at Ivigtut on the 22d of May in two flocks of about one dozen each. As Dr. Oesterbye found them on July 15, 1888, at the so-called " bird-cliff " of Kangarsuk, about 62° N., it may be that they breed there.

RAZOR-BILLED AUK.

ALCA TORDA.

This I have not seen at Ivigtut; but, according to Dr. Oesterbye, about five hundred pair breed at the above-named " bird-cliff," whence I obtained its eggs and a skin.

DOVEKIE.

ALLE ALLE.

A winter visitor, not common at Ivigtut, but at times abundant about Arsuk. In the fall of 1886, it arrived at the same time as Brünnich's Murre, with which it often associates. One day sixty-five Murres and two Dovekies were shot from the edge of the ice, — which gives approximately their relative numbers. In 1888 no Dovekies were seen about Arsuk after the close of March.

PARASITIC JAEGER.

STERCORARIUS PARASITICUS.

Two examples — one a dark bird, the other with a light-colored body — were often seen in the summer of 1888 over the fjord, hunting the Kittiwakes. They probably had a nest in the neighborhood.

IVORY GULL.

GAVIA ALBA.

On the 1st of June, during a southeast rainstorm, I observed one on the fjord among the Kittiwakes. Formerly quite a number were shot about Ivigtut. I obtained two skins of old birds and one of a young bird, all taken near Ivigtut some few years ago.

KITTIWAKE.

RISSA TRIDACTYLA.

I saw examples of this species about the vessel every day during my voyage from the Shetland Islands to Greenland.

The arrival of these birds at Ivigtut and their departure was noticed as follows: In 1886, last seen October 23, a few. In 1887, first seen, March 26, a large flock; last seen, October 25, a few. In 1888, first seen, April 9, a large flock; at my departure, October 17, still common.

From their arrival till the middle of May they keep together in one or more large flocks, and are then very timid and noisy. This is, perhaps, because the fjord is to a great extent covered with ice, so that their nesting-ground lies eight to ten miles from open water. On clear days in April a flock of some two thousand may be seen rising to a great height, say three thousand to four thousand feet, sometimes going out of sight, so that one can only hear their screeching as they rapidly wheel about. They are then wont to make an excursion inland, above the ice, toward their breeding-place. On returning, they descend somewhat more scattered; but at once on reaching the water, they gather close together. These exercises they often go through many times a day

In May they assemble in smaller flocks, and are less shy. About two thousand lay their eggs on the front of a perpendicular cliff situated at the head of the fjord. The lowest nests may easily be reached from a boat; the highest are about one hundred and fifty feet above the sea. The eggs are laid chiefly during the first ten days of June, and the young fly from their nests about the middle of August. (The earliest date on which I have seen a young bird is the 7th of August.) After that they generally go about in small flocks or singly, and keep comparatively silent. On a few occasions only, on August afternoons, I have seen large flocks of five hundred to one thousand individuals rise to a great height and fly toward the ocean.

During the autumn these Gulls have a daily route, — in the morning, inland along the fjord, and in the afternoon out along the fjord toward the sea; where they probably remain over night. This is directly opposite to the custom of the Eider Duck in winter, and of the large young Gulls in summer; these fly up the fjord — inland — as night approaches. Some days, especially when rain is falling and the wind is high, they fly rather near the shore; but usually not nearer than five hundred feet. Only twice have I seen them sitting on land, except at their nests. On one occasion I saw a single bird, probably a sick one, alight on the shore; and again, on the 3d of June, I saw a number of Gulls plucking moss on the cliffs along the fjord, about nine miles distant from their nesting-ground, and then fly about without any apparent object, holding the moss in their bills. What they meant by this I could not understand, for there was plenty of moss in the neighborhood of their nests.

During June the Gulls feed to a great extent on a small fish (*Mallotus arcticus*) which comes to the surface in vast numbers. They also follow whales and seals. By throwing

a dead or wounded Gull out of a boat, they may easily be
brought within shooting distance.

GLAUCOUS GULL

LARUS GLAUCUS.

This species breeds in considerable numbers along the
open sea; and probably, also, high up on the "bird-cliff"
at the head of the fjord, — above the nests of *Larus leucopterus.* Some, chiefly young birds, remain over winter. An
old bird, in a complete summer dress, was shot on the 20th
of March. I have seen these Gulls enter, uninvited, among
the Eider Ducks, and try to rob them of mussels that they
had brought up from the bottom. After the young leave
their nests in August, they gather on the flat tracts along
the shore, and feed on the berries of *Empetrum nigrum*, of
which they consume a vast quantity. At this time the
young birds are by no means shy, while the old birds are
always difficult to approach.

ICELAND GULL.

LARUS LEUCOPTERUS.

A number of young birds, and some few old ones, remain during the winter, but the majority leave in October
and return in March. About a thousand pair nest on the
"bird-cliff," above the Kittiwakes. The lowest nests are
built at a height of about two hundred feet; the highest at
about five hundred feet above sea-level. In 1888 a single
pair hatched their young away from the rest, on the face of
the cliff, close by the edge of the ice, and at the height of
forty feet. Two pair raised their young, during the three
summers I was in Greenland, on a cliff which was formerly

the home of numerous Kittiwakes. One of these nests was at the height of fifteen feet, the other one hundred feet above sea-level.

These Gulls often lay their eggs while the fjord below is still covered with ice. Some few young fly from their nests at the close of July. The earliest date that I have seen young birds was on July 25, but the main body did not appear until the earlier part of August. For a while after leaving the nests, they are accompanied by one of the parents, or by both, and these give warning in a wise and unmistakable manner; "Don't go near those treacherous boats," they seem to cry. Later on the young mingle with the young of the Glaucous Gull, but not with young Kittiwakes.

The young Iceland Gulls feed on the berries of *Empetrum nigrum*, rest frequently on land or on the ice, and are not at all timid. In voice and habits the young birds quite resemble young Glaucous Gulls. When at the nesting-ground the old birds utter a cry resembling *kee* in a loud harsh tone.

GREAT BLACK-BACKED GULL.

LARUS MARINUS.

Found in very small numbers at all seasons of the year, but most numerous in the fall. Old, faded birds are but rarely seen. As a rule these Gulls are extremely shy.

FULMAR.

FULMARUS GLACIALIS.

Occurs at times in great numbers a few miles off the coast, and is said to enter the fjord occasionally. On my voyages to and from Greenland they were seen daily in greater or less numbers, all the way from the Shetland

Islands to within a few miles of Greenland. They fed on meat and other refuse thrown from the vessel. I observed that they always alighted on the water before taking the food, and if it had sunk under the surface, they would dive for it to the depth of about two feet. By means of a line I caught one, which I kept on board for about ten days, during which time it took no food to my knowledge.

As we sighted Greenland I saw the largest flock, and among these were a large number that were dark-colored, of which I had seen but few previously on the voyage. On the stretch between 36° and 20° W. there was among these Fulmars a number of Shearwaters, which I supposed to be *Puffinus puffinus.*

LEACH'S PETREL.

OCEANODROMA LEUCORHOA.

Is said to have been seen occasionally near Arsuk.

CORMORANT.

PHALACROCORAX CARBO.

Not uncommon about Arsuk in winter until the end of April, but seldom goes as far into the fjord as Ivigtut. Its skin is much prized by furriers.

RED-BREASTED MERGANSER.

MERGANSER SERRATOR.

Common during the spring migration, but is also met with during the winter. I have known of examples being shot in November, December, and February. These birds are generally found singly, though sometimes two or three are together.

As I have several times seen it about Ivigtut in summer, I suppose it nests in that neighborhood.

MALLARD.

ANAS BOSCHAS.

Common the whole year round, but most numerous in winter, when they keep in small flocks along the shore. One or two pair breed in the swampy portion of the valley near Ivigtut. Nests with eggs were found June 27, 1886, and May 31, 1888. Two ducklings a few days old were caught June 26, 1887, early in the morning, one in the village, the other in the harbor. The mother had probably brought them along a small river that flows through the town.

The eggs of the Greenland Mallard are considerably larger than those of the Danish bird; the former measure 60 mm. by 44 mm.; the latter 56 mm. by 41 mm.

BARROW'S GOLDEN-EYE.

GLAUCIONETTA ISLANDICA.

A male was shot at Ivigtut March 23, 1887, and the same year, on April 12, I observed two males and one female. It must be rare in these parts, as neither Danes nor Greenlanders know it.

OLD SQUAW.

CLANGULA HYEMALIS.

Very common about Arsuk from October to the end of April, but shows itself only rarely on the fjord near Ivigtut.

3

HARLEQUIN DUCK.

HISTRIONICUS HISTRIONICUS.

Breeds in several places. Arrives in April and remains
until early in November (Nov. 5, 1887). On August 28,
I observed half-grown young on the fjord. During summer
the males gather in small flocks on the fjord.

NORTHERN EIDER.

SOMATERIA MOLLISSIMA BOREALIS.

Breeds in great numbers on the islets by the open sea.
In the winter great flocks gather on the fjord near Ivigtut.
In June, 1886, I observed in the course of an hour between
five hundred and a thousand Eiders on the fjord in flocks of
about fifty. Each flock consisted chiefly of females, accompanied by a few males. In the evening they went up the
fjord as in winter, but did not go as far inland. The two
following summers I observed a few times smaller compa-
nies of females and an occasional male on the fjord.

Holboll also met with flocks of unmated birds in summer,
far from their nesting-sites, and observed that the two sexes
generally kept separate from each other; also, that there
were more flocks of males than of females, and that in the
beginning of the breeding-season these flocks were of small
size. From this he concluded that these flocks consisted of
birds which had either lost their mates or their young.

My observations during the summers of 1887 and 1888
might indeed go to strengthen Holboll's hypothesis, but it
does not seem to me that the mere presence of numbers
of these Ducks on the fjord at a great distance from their
breeding-ground in the beginning of the season of 1886
need necessarily be due to the causes suggested by Holboll.

I am rather inclined to believe that their nesting was delayed that year by the big ice which then enclosed some of their principal resorts as late as June.

In October, 1886, the females began to come into the fjord singly, and in November they came in small flocks. As the weather grew colder the number increased, and it became still larger after Christmas, the period of greatest abundance being March and April. The males did not come in as great numbers into the fjord that winter. I saw, indeed, none at Ivigtut until March, while they were quite numerous at Christmas of the following year.

In the evening these birds generally go as far inland as there is open water, and during the night they are almost constantly on the move. Then their cries may be plainly heard, as also their splashing near the shore; but if a match be lit, they fly aloft with a great uproar.

KING EIDER.

SOMATERIA SPECTABILIS.

An example of this species was first observed by me on Feb. 1, 1887. By the 12th of that month they had arrived in great numbers; and from the middle of the month until the middle of March they were even more numerous than the common Eider Ducks; but from that time on *spectabilis* decreased, while *borealis* increased. By the middle of April there were but few King Eiders left, and the last obtained was shot on the 29th of that month.

In habits the present species much resembles *borealis*, but seeks rather deeper water, and is oftener-seen resting in a standing posture on the brink of the ice. Its only note is a single cooing sound, heard especially at night. Like the common Eider, these birds are very shy and difficult to shoot.

The easiest method of getting within shooting distance of a
flock is by hiding behind a snow-bank, near the edge of the
ice, where they congregate.

PURPLE SANDPIPER.

TRINGA MARITIMA.

Common on the shores of Arsuk fjord from the beginning
of October throughout the winter. As I have observed some
examples in the same locality during summer, they may
have nested in the vicinity.

PECTORAL SANDPIPER.

TRINGA MACULATA.

In the autumn of 1886 I obtained one skin of this species,
that had been taken at Frederickshaab. It is now in the
zoölogical museum at Copenhagen.

WHIMBREL.

NUMENIUS PHÆOPUS.

One was shot at Arsuk May 25, 1887 ; I also obtained the
skin of one shot at Ivigtut a few years before.

AMERICAN GOLDEN PLOVER.

CHARADRIUS DOMINICUS.

I obtained the skin of one shot at Frederickshaab in the
autumn of 1886, and gave it to the zoölogical museum at
Copenhagen.

RING PLOVER.
AEGIALITIS HIATICULA.

Examples of this species were seen on Aug. 15, 1886, beside a lake at the height of eleven hundred feet.

REINHARDT'S PTARMIGAN.
LAGOPUS RUPESTRIS REINHARDTI.

Breeds usually about Ivigtut. During winter the number is considerably increased by the birds coming from the north, but the abundance is very variable. Thus the first winter I was at Ivigtut, an uncommonly cold season, comparatively few were seen, though about four hundred were shot; but the following winter, which was much milder, the birds were much more numerous, and about twice as many were killed. When snow covers the ground they are less frequent in the valleys than on the mountain slopes and in the clefts; but on the high lands they are not so numerous. They usually resort to side hills, where there are large bowlders, and where some herbs are easily accessible. They change their feeding-ground very often, and sometimes in the course of a single night they arrive in such numbers that on the following day the birds or their tracks may be seen everywhere, while at other times one may travel for days without seeing any sign of one.

Usually, and especially in calm weather, these birds are far from shy; only in windy weather is it sometimes difficult to approach them within shot-range.

They usually are met with in small flocks of six or so, and often none but a single bird or a pair are in sight. I think the largest flock I ever saw numbered but thirteen. When the snow is soft, they often dig tunnels, in which they pass the night. Twice it happened that Ptarmigans came from across the ice-covered fjord in the morning, and alighted on the roofs of the houses, where of course they were shot.

It is very interesting to see a flock of Ptarmigans walking about in the snow, and with subdued murmurs hunting for food. They generally sit still while one approaches them, trusting, no doubt, that their white coat will protect them from being discovered; but their black bills and dark eyes, and the black stripe on the males, render them quite conspicuous. Several times when I have come upon them in summer they have retreated to the nearest snow-field, apparently forgetting that they wore their winter costume no longer. They often let their voice be heard, and then the males and the females may be distinguished.

The females do not don their summer dress until June, and the males much later, — perhaps more than a month. On the 1st of July they were still half-white; and on the 20th of July I saw a male that was white on the breast. By the 20th of September both sexes are about half-white and half-gray, and when October closes most of them are attired in their winter costume. The old birds regain their winter color earlier than do the younger.

Three times I found female Ptarmigans with their young in the month of July. On the 20th of July I found one at the height of thirteen hundred feet, with her young yet quite small. The mother was exceedingly anxious about her brood, and ran so close to my feet that I could easily have struck her with my walking-stick. The chicks ran away faster than I could have walked, and seemed to have a surprisingly good idea of how to hide themselves, although there was really nothing to cover them. The cries of the mother were of a guttural tone, while the piping of the young resembled that of some chickens. The same day

I met a pair whose actions suggested that they had lost their young.

On the 26th and the 29th of July I saw two female Ptar-migans with their broods at the height of a hundred feet and a thousand feet respectively. One brood was half grown, the other somewhat older.

GRAY SEA EAGLE.

HALIÆETUS ALBICILLA.

Common, nesting in all suitable places. It is most numer-ous in winter, especially when north winds prevail. On one occasion I saw twelve Eagles and again fourteen on the fjord. I frequently observed them pursuing my Doves, though these did not seem to fear their pursuers, but would rather tanta-lize them by circling around them. On one occasion one of these Eagles tried to get some liver which was being trolled after a boat, as bait for Gulls. As it did so, a shot was fired at it, but it escaped unhurt. A short time after it came again, and had then to pay with its life for the foolhardy venture. Usually, however, they are very shy and difficult of approach. I secured two clutches of two eggs each; and on the 20th of July some natives took from a nest an almost full-fledged eaglet, which was fed on fish for some time.

WHITE GYRFALCON.

FALCO ISLANDUS.

GRAY GYRFALCON.

FALCO RUSTICOLUS.

I have examined about thirty skins of the Greenland Gyr-falcon, — some of them in the meat, — all shot in South

Greenland, and have thus had an opportunity to decide with tolerable certainty to which of the species they belonged. The distinguishing characteristics adopted by Mr. Ridgway in his Manual cannot, in my opinion, be considered reliable. One specimen, which by its general color was certainly of the white form, had the under tail-coverts slightly marked by dusky spots, and this specimen, as well as about half the other white Falcons, had dark spots on their thighs, while an occasional bird had almost as dark color on the thighs and ventral region as *F. rusticolus*. As Holboll and Fencker repeatedly observed mated pairs, one of which was white (*F. islandicus*), and the other dark (*F. rusticolus*), and as Holboll also found light and dark colored young in the same nest, I conclude with these observers that there is but one species of Gyrfalcon found in Greenland; that the light-colored birds breed chiefly in North Greenland, while the dark birds are chiefly restricted to South Greenland; and, further, I believe that the two forms are related much in the same way as those of the *Fulmariæ*, some forms of *Stercorarius*, and the mammalian *Canus lagopus*. I have in my possession the skins of two white female Gyrfalcons shot during the breeding-season in April and May at Fredericks-haab, in South Greenland.

Besides, it seems to me unfortunate that these forms should be ranked as species merely on the strength of data furnished by dried skins, without taking the habits and other characteristics of the living birds into consideration. Especially do Mr. Holboll's observations seem to me valuable in settling this question.

The following table exhibits the result of my observations of the Gyrfalcon during my stay in Greenland. It is divided into three columns, the first giving the number of white birds observed, the second the number of those whose color

I was not able to determine, while the third column gives the number of the gray-colored birds.

	1886.			1887.			1888.		
	White.	Undet.	Gray.	White.	Undet.	Gray.	White.	Undet.	Gray.
January . .	...	...	...	8	2	2	10	1	1
February . .	...	...	...	...	...	...	2		
March . . .	...	...	...	...	2	...	1	1	
April . . .	...	...	...	2	1	1			
May									
June	...	...	1						
July	...	...	...	...	...	...	...	1	
August . . .	...	...	1	...	...	3	...	...	1
September .	...	...	...	1	1	2	1	1	1
October . .	...	...	...	6	2	2	...	1	
November . .	4	1	...	6	1				
December . .	12-16	2-3	1	1	1				

That their abundance in winter varies with the weather I am not in a position to decide, but think that more prob-ably depends on the number and the movements of the Ptar-migans, their principal food at that season.

In the winter I used to take my Pigeons out every day, so that when Falcons came in sight I might induce them to come within shooting-range; but I have to confess that, owing to their great swiftness, I much oftener missed than hit them. The young Pigeons sought security almost any-where, even in the sitting-room; but the old birds often tried to escape by rising in the air, sometimes flying so high that both Pigeon and Falcon were for a time lost to sight; and so swift and skilled on the wing were they that I did not lose a single Pigeon. Occasionally the Falcons tried to catch a Pigeon that was sitting on the roof of the house, but always in vain. On the other hand the Falcons themselves were at times worried by Ravens, but neither party seemed ever to be in real earnest.

Once a Falcon was attracted by the report of my gun as I shot a Ptarmigan, and I brought him within shot-range by throwing the dead Ptarmigan into the air. At another time I observed a white Falcon sitting at some distance from a dark Falcon, that was making his repast on a sea-fowl, and when the dark Falcon flew away with his prey the white one followed, evidently hoping to obtain a portion.

I have at various times heard these birds utter somewhat weak and tremulous cries, resembling sounds I have heard from *Falco tinnunculus.*

In summer the present species is less frequently seen near the settlements in the vicinity of Ivigtut; but it nests nevertheless in the neighborhood of the " bird-cliff." On the 3d of June, 1886, there was shot a dark Falcon, with a naked spot on the ventral side, and in its stomach were found the remains of a Ptarmigan.

From Frederickshaab I obtained a set of eggs said to have been gathered on the 16th of April, while the ground was under a mantle of snow.

Measured transversely, the white and the gray Falcons are of about the same size; namely, 59 to 60 cm. long, on the average. The largest I measured was 62 cm. long and 133 cm. broad, and weighed 1.8 kilogram. The smallest, a gray specimen, was 51.5 cm. long, 102 cm. broad, and weighed 0.9 kilogram; and a white bird measured about the same length.

[The observations recorded here suggest that the gray and white forms of the Greenland Gyrfalcons are merely individual differences, — phases of plumage, — instead of being specific, as assumed by many systematists. The mating of gray and white birds, and the occurrence of young birds of both colors in one nest, certainly point in that direction.

If, however, as Mr. Hagerup thinks, the white-colored birds are mainly found in summer in North Greenland, while those breeding in the southern section usually wear the darker plumage, then the two might be ranked as geographical races.

The suggestions are interesting, but the evidence offered is too slight to assist materially in solving the problem that these birds present to scientific ornithologists.—M. C.]

DUCK HAWK.

FALCO PEREGRINUS ANATUM.

I have not seen a single living example of this species at Ivigtut, only the skin of one shot a few years ago. From Frederickshaab I obtained the skins of two young birds shot in the fall of 1886, also the skin of an adult female shot April 21, 1888, at her nest, which contained two eggs. Besides this I obtained one egg taken on the 1st of May, 1888.

This species is said to be much more dangerous to the Pigeons than is the Gyrfalcon.

SNOWY OWL.

NYCTEA NYCTEA.

A rare winter visitor. In January, 1886, a fine Owl almost wholly white was taken. When wounded it attacked the man who shot it.

NORTHERN RAVEN.

CORVUS CORAX PRINCIPALIS.

Very common all the year round; seen and heard daily along the coast.

From August to October they gather in flocks, sometimes as many as thirty, or in families. About this time they feed largely on the berries of *Empetrum nigrum*, of which they consume a great quantity.

Often one Raven or more would attend the Eagles, as they sat on the ice devouring their prey, and would even make it unpleasant for the latter.

At first the Ravens tried to pursue my Pigeons, but they soon gave that up as useless. On one occasion, however, a Raven pursued a Pigeon with surprising perseverance. At last I lost sight of both, and never saw the Pigeon again.

The Ravens often give the trappers considerable trouble, for they are cunning enough to take the bait out of the fox-trap and get their head out of the way before the trap falls upon them. But occasionally they lose their heads in the trap. I once caught a Raven instead of a fox in one of those old-fashioned stone-traps in which a piece of board loaded with a stone falls as soon as the bait is touched, and crushes the victim. They are very noisy and curious, and if one stands still on the mountain-cliffs, especially if he has a dog with him, the Ravens will often come close to him, within easy shooting-distance.

I frequently noticed that when a strong wind blew from the north they migrated in great numbers toward the south. The largest of these migrations took place August 30, 1887, when one hundred to two hundred crossed the valley. They were seen through the entire day coming from the north side of the fjord, flying low over it, stopping a little at the south shore, then crossing the valley until they reached the mountains. At the base of the hills they first began to rise in the air, working upwards in spiral curves without any flapping of wings, until abreast of the summit, when they sailed away to the south.

They are usually found almost everywhere; soaring above the fjord; walking along the shore; about the houses; up on the highlands, where no means of subsistence is apparent,—even many miles in the interior, above the lifeless mer-de-glace.

I saw nests at different heights, ranging from twenty to one thousand feet above sea-level, on inaccessible cliffs facing the fjord near Ivigtut.

At Frederickshaab I obtained four sets of three to four eggs each. These were taken between the 11th and the 28th of April. I think it builds among the earliest of any species found in that region. On the 19th of June I saw some full-fledged young close by the "bird-cliff," where the parents most likely fed them.

GREATER REDPOLL.

ACANTHIS LINARIA ROSTRATA.

The most numerous of the smaller birds found in the vicinity of Ivigtut. In 1886 it was first observed on May 6, and was common on May 17. On September 24 the majority had migrated southward, though a few were met with now and then during October. On the 26th of October, when the country was covered with snow a foot deep, three or four were seen, but none were seen during November. On the 5th of December, however, one was discovered, and on the 8th five or six appeared, and of the latter some wore red on the breast. On the following day I saw two in the

same place, hunting for food among a few bushes that pro-
jected above the snow along the edge of the fjord, which at
that time was covered with ice.

In 1887, the first were seen on April 24, and on April 30
a few single individuals, besides three together flying toward
west-northwest, about one hundred feet high. On the 6th
of May several appeared in the valley, and by the 10th of the
same month, they were common. By September 28, most of
the flock had migrated, but a few were seen in October, and
one on November 21.

In 1888 one with a red breast was seen on the 27th of
January, and one on the 4th of February. The latter were
seen in the same bushes where I had found those on the
8th and 9th of December, 1886, and, as then, the weather
was mild and the whole country covered with snow. On
the 10th of May, 1888, the time of mating, they were quite
common.

These birds usually build wherever a bunch of bushes
may be found, but rarely over five hundred or six hundred
feet up the hillside, although I have met examples on the
higher lands during the mating-season. I discovered eight
nests with eggs and young. Three of the nests had the full
number of eggs in May, the others in June. The earliest
newly-laid eggs were found on May 20, the latest on June
26. One clutch consisted of four eggs, another of six, and
the remainder of five eggs or young.

These nests were in willow bushes, generally in the lowest branches, close to the ground, and never higher than
three and one half feet. An exception was a nest built
upon one of the seats in an old boat which lay beside a
thoroughfare within the town of Ivigtut. On the 26th of
June there were four eggs in the nest, and on the 4th of
July there were, I believe, young in the nest, but I am not

quite sure, for the old bird would not stir from the nest, although I touched it, and I had not the heart to drive it away by force. But the young escaped all harm, as far as I know, so long as they remained in the nest, although it was often visited by people passing.

I was told that a short time before a pair of Redpolls had for two years in succession hatched their young in a bird-cage that hung outside a building about nine feet from the ground, the wires being so far apart as to permit the birds passing between them.

The nests which I found were made chiefly of dried grass and roots, the inside being lined with white plant-wool, and often with a few Ptarmigan feathers, so that it looked altogether white.

At the end of June, when the willows are in leaf, the young forsake their nests. During July and August and the first half of September, both old and young used to come about the houses, gathering in flocks on the refuse heaps outside the brewery, and, if then a cage with a decoy bird was placed near them, they were easily caught in a net. Some were caught as they flew into the houses hunting for relatives already captured. Within a few days I caught in a net as many as twenty. They were easily tamed, and often ate from the hand, even on the first day of their captivity.

Once I gave some their liberty, after keeping them four-teen days as prisoners; but they returned to the cage after a few hours' or a day's absence; and when I let them fly about the room to catch flies, I could lure them to sit on my hand by holding out a bit of hemp to them. I fed them chiefly on groats steeped in water.

When caged they became a little quarrelsome, especially the red-breasted males, obliging me to separate one of these

from the rest for fear of his injuring, or perhaps killing
them.   They are usually sociable, even during the nesting-
season.

When a flock is approached one sounds a note of warning,
which generally attracts a dozen who call out like the first,
though they soon fall to singing and teasing one another,
showing but little fear of the disturber, and often flying or
hopping within six feet of him.   Then, all of a sudden, some
one calls " time," and in a wink they are away.   They are
always restless, — always on the go.   During the summer
they live to a great extent on insects, and one which I shot
on the 2d of July had its œsophagus full of small flies.

Their song, which they deliver both when flying and perch-
ing, is but ordinary, and consists mostly of trills, reminding
one of the song of *Fringilla chloris.*

I tried to examine their various garbs and moulting, both
on some thirty captured birds and on wild ones, but have
not yet come to any final conclusion in that matter.   During
the winter, from the close of November to May, I did not
keep any birds captive, and my identification of the sexes
was based chiefly on difference of voice and color.

Their usual *summer garb*, worn during the hatching-season,
and until the beginning of July, is a uniform dark-gray one
on the back, the sides gray with white stripes, a blackish
fleck on the throat, a blackish bill, and a crown of crimson.
About seven per cent are tinged with a rosy color on the
upper tail-coverts, and especially on the breast.   A few had
also a reddish tint on the malar region, though otherwise
darker colored.   The males which I saw at the nests had
red crests, but were nowhere else red-colored.

The moulting begins in July or August, and then the
birds lose all this red color, even the brightest-colored
males.   In the autumn dress, which they then obtain, they

are of a much lighter color and display more yellow, — not, indeed, that the feathers are of a uniform yellow on the back, but they are variegated with lighter and darker streaks of yellowish-brown. The greater coverts form a broader, the lesser coverts a narrower flaxen-colored stripe. The wing-feathers are light-colored on the edges; the sides of the body speckled brown; the under side a light yellowish-gray; the throat-fleck blackish; the crown bronze. This was the plumage of ten old birds, which I caught either in full summer garb, or immediately after the moulting had begun.

One bright-colored male, which I caught on the 16th of July, had already begun to moult on the crown; only a third part of it remained red, while the rest was of a bronze color. The moulting was so slow that in November it had still some red left in its crown, and the only thing it had yet obtained of the autumn dress was the light-colored stripes on the wings, and on some of its flight feathers; but it still retained its dark color on the breast. Its dress looked, however, somewhat worn and faded, compared with the colors of its companions. When caught, it seemed as if a portion of the bill was about to fall off; for it was partly covered with a rough horny mass of a darker color. After a couple of days this horny mass had disappeared, but I could not find it in the cage. The bill was then somewhat lighter colored, and somewhat weaker than the bills of the other Redpolls; it was hardly strong enough to break a hemp seed. This circumstance, as well as the slow moulting, indicates perhaps that the bird was sick, although it seemed in other respects quite as lively as the rest.

Another pretty red-breasted male, caught on June 20, moulted in July, and obtained the usual autumn dress with its yellow crown. Just after the young birds have left their nests, they are of a somewhat dark gray color on the back but light gray on the under side, with many longish and dark colored stripes, but no dark fleck on the throat. They moult at the same time as the old birds, in July and August, and attain the usual autumn dress in every detail, with this difference in some of them, however, that the crown becomes quite dark-red, or copper-colored, with far less metallic lustre than that of the old birds during the summer.

Those birds which I have caught in the fall after the moulting have, as a rule, been rather lighter colored and more yellowish than those that moulted in captivity, and have, besides, had a more lustrous bronze or copper-colored crown.

From the following noted circumstance it would appear that some birds keep their autumn dress during the whole summer, and presumably also during the mating and nesting season. On the 17th of May, 1886, I saw among the newly arrived birds, all of which had a red crown, one or two birds which had no red on the crown, but had a darker colored head, and a faintly red-speckled breast. I also caught two birds in full autumn dress with yellowish-bronze colored crowns, one on the 1st of July, the other on the 23d of May. This last was a male, a great and good singer, and very attentive to the females who were his imprisoned companions. These two birds did not moult during the whole summer.

My observations on the moulting of these birds in captivity convinced me that all old birds, from the brightest-colored male to the dullest-colored female, lose their red color completely during the autumn moulting (or it might be called the summer moulting), and then quite resemble the young as they appear after their first moult, excepting that some of the latter get a copper-colored crown. Never-

theless I have seen in autumn and winter birds that had,
besides reddish crowns, pale red or pink colored breasts, and
were otherwise in common autumn dress.

It might be supposed either that these birds have obtained
the red color after moulting, or that some of my captive
birds, on account of their captivity, as well as the change of
food (I fed them chiefly on barley-meal and hemp-seed),
obtained a different color from what they would have borne
had they been free. I may add that the birds I saw in winter seemed to me rather lighter than those I had seen during
the autumn.

[It is well known that many birds do not resume their
brightest colors after moulting when in captivity. — M. C.]

HOUSE SPARROW.
PASSER DOMESTICUS.

A few of these Sparrows were introduced here some years
ago. During the first few winters they fed on oats; and
in the summer laid their eggs in boxes placed outside the
houses. On my arrival in 1886 there were only five males
left, and in 1888 only two, so there seems no immediate
danger of Greenland being overrun with Sparrows, as has
been the fate of the United States and Canada.

What has acted so injuriously upon the Sparrows here is
— so I believe — not so much the severe cold, as the long-
continued storms of cold wind, accompanied by snow and
rain.

SNOWFLAKE.
PLECTROPHENAX NIVALIS.

This merry songster is abundant in summer, but I have
never seen it in winter, — neither in the valleys nor on the

highlands, where, according to Holboll, a great number pass the winter.

In 1886, when I arrived, it was common on the 22d of April, and loud in its songs. On the 15th of October the greater number had left Ivigtut; the last were seen on the 25th of October.

In 1887, the first, a single one, was seen on the 30th of March, then one on April 3, and five or six on the following day. On April 8, a flock of twenty to thirty was seen, and a week later single individuals were observed; but they were not common until April 23. The last were seen on the 17th of October.

In 1888 the first, a single one, was seen on the 5th of April; on the 7th and the following days a number were observed; and from the 13th of April on, they were common. On the 5th of May a flock of about forty was seen among the bushes in the valley, where they have not been seen at other times. On the 15th of October they were still common.

I have found six nests with eggs or young, always six in each. The earliest eggs were found on the 26th of May, the last on June the 14th. The nests were generally at an elevation of fifty to three hundred feet above sea-level; but I have also found the birds, though rarely, during the hatching-season, as high as two thousand feet in the uplands.

Their favored hatching-places are the mountain slopes, where numerous stone-heaps afford them a convenient place for nest-building. On one occasion I noticed a male coming about every five minutes to a bright sunny spot, where it caught a few blue-bottles, and then flew away in a definite direction. By following it, I found about fifteen hundred feet distant a nest with some half-grown young.

All the nests I saw were built between stones, sometimes far in among the heaps, and occasionally I was obliged to roll several large stones away in order to get at the nests. One nest had been used for one or more years previously. It was very large, and the outside consisted of a mass of damp moss and portions of plants, as well as some feathers. Within this came a layer half an inch thick, made of straw and a few tufts of fox-hair; but the innermost part consisted of white Ptarmigan feathers, one Raven's feather, and a few fox-hairs.

The males were usually very anxious about their nests, and often uttered an agreeable and clear but melancholy note; but the mothers were generally very trustful, and often flew with insects into their nests while I stood by and looked on.

During the hatching-season, they live in pairs for a couple of weeks before they lay their eggs. In July and August the young are often seen in flocks about the houses.

It is chiefly in April, while the country is still covered with snow, that their glorious song is most appreciated. It consists of loud and clear flute-notes combined into short stanzas, but has no definite melody. The birds sing frequently while sitting on an elevation, but seldom on the wing.

LAPLAND LONGSPUR.

CALCARIUS LAPPONICUS.

The least common of our songsters. In 1886 it was first seen May 24. In 1887 the first was seen on May 22; the last on August 30. In 1888 the first was seen on May 20, and the birds were common on the 23d of May. The last was seen on the 30th of August.

It is only found in damp places covered with grass and scattered bushes; and I never observed it higher than two hundred feet above sea-level.

In the Ivigtut valley, which is about one third of an English square mile in area, there hatched about eight to ten pair in 1886, and in 1887, and in the following year about twice as many. In numbers it bears the following ratio to our other small birds : one to five of *Saxicola œnanthe ;* one to twenty, *Plectrophenax nivalis ;* one to thirty, *Acanthis linaria.*

On the 16th of June, 1887, I chanced to find a nest (as the mother flew away), located deep down in the moss at the foot of a willow bush. On the outside it was made of stalks of herbs and of roots, while the inside was made of white Ptarmigan feathers. It contained seven fresh-laid eggs. On the 3d of July my dog caught a chick, that was still scarcely able to fly.

The parents are exceedingly anxious about their nests, and one can hear the male bird's sweet but sad *tloo*, and other notes of alarm, even while several hundred feet away.

The song, which sounds best while the birds descend slowly and without flapping of wings from on high, is but short, and of an extremely melancholy nature, but contains very pretty warbling runs, which are always repeated ·in the same order, and in a comparatively slow time. It does not sing very often.

WHEATEAR.

SAXICOLA ŒNANTHE.

Is common, and builds its nest in all suitable places. In 1886 the first was observed on the 5th of May, and the last were seen on the 5th of October, none having been noticed for several weeks previous. In 1887 the first were seen on the 12th of May, — and the males sang cheerfully, — though on the previous day I had looked for them in vain. The last were seen on the 25th of September. In 1888 the first was seen on the 16th of May, the last on the 23d of September.

It builds its nest in similar places to the Snow Bunting, at a depth of six inches to four feet, or even more. I have found several nests at an elevation ranging from three feet to seven hundred above sea-level, and with six, seven, or eight eggs. The first-laid eggs were found June 3; the latest date was June 28.

The nests contain, on the average, one egg more than those found in Denmark. One pair utilized the same nest for two successive years. It was built in the stone wall which surrounded the powder-magazine. During the hatching-season I have seen them in pairs at a height of twelve hundred feet on the highlands.

This bird seems to have learned one tune from the Snow Bunting, for at the nests both males and females may be heard to whistle a tune which can hardly be distinguished from that of the Snow Bunting on similar occasions; but I have never heard the Danish Wheatears whistle that tune.

[It is probable that the Greenland Wheatear is sufficiently distinct to merit varietal rank.

Besides the difference in habits noted by the present author, we have the report of Mr. Howard Saunders that the Greenland birds have been observed to perch on trees much more than is the habit of the English-bred birds; and several writers have recorded the opinion that specimens from Greenland averaged a larger size than those taken in Europe. — M. C.]

CATALOGUE

OF

THE BIRDS OF GREENLAND.

THE following Catalogue is based on the works of Holboll, Reinhardt, Alfred Newton, Ludwig Kumlien, and
others; use has also been made of the late Alfred Benzon's
collection of bird-skins and eggs.   By utilizing abundant
material gathered by Benzon, who for a number of years
received eggs and skins of birds from the various settlements in Greenland, and by adding thereto my own observations, I am able to present a more complete record than
has been given in any list hitherto published on the birds of
Greenland, especially as regards their breeding-seasons.   I
have also been able to add two species which had not been
discovered before in Greenland.

The Catalogue comprises all the birds discovered up to
date in that part of western Greenland which is settled by
Danes ; namely, the country lying south of 73° N. lat.
This is divided at 68° N. lat. into North Greenland and
South Greenland.

As it is often impossible to determine to what variety a
bird belongs by merely examining its eggs, and as the eggs
and skins which Mr. Benzon obtained from Greenland were
collected chiefly by men who lacked ornithological knowledge, I have made it a rule, in using his material, to pay no

heed whatever to the statements made in the Catalogue regarding eggs, unless these have also been identified by other
naturalists. Thus, for example, the following is entered in
the Benzon Catalogue:—

Eggs of *Uria troile* (two eggs from Julianeshaab); *Gavia
alba* (one egg from Greenland — Holboll) ; *Aythya marila*
(one hatch of eggs from Christianshaab, 1872); *Chen hyper-
borea* (two hatches of eggs from Egedesminde, 1875); *Branta
leucopsis* (one egg from Egedesminde); *Numenius borealis* (?)
(one egg from Egedesminde, 1865).

On the other hand, when I have found sufficient data in
Benzon's Catalogue and in my own notes from Greenland,
I have added the dates when the eggs were found first, and
when last.

I would also note that when a bird is said to breed "everywhere," I mean, of course, in any suitable locality.

I have noted here only unpublished reports regarding the
occurrence of the rarer birds in Greenland, and for further
information I must ask my readers to consult the works of
the authors named above.

---

1. Holboll's Grebe. (*Colymbus holbœllii.*)

Occasional visitor.

2. Horned Grebe. (*Colymbus auritus.*)

Occasional visitor. Benzon obtained the skin of a young
bird taken at Godthaab, 1877.

[Reinhardt reports taking one example of this species in
young plumage, and Newton states that a " few immature
specimens have been obtained in the southern part of Greenland." We might expect to find it breeding there, as eggs
taken on the Yukon River are in the National Museum at

Washington, and the birds have been taken on the Lower
Mackenzie as well as in Iceland, Northern Norway, and
Siberia. — M. C.]

[NOTE. — The Black-throated Diver (*Urinator arcticus*)
has been taken in Parry's Sound, Grinnell Bay, and King-
wah Fjord, and probably occurs on the Greenland shore, but
there is no evidence of it having been seen there. — M. C.]

3. Loon. (*Urinator imber.*)

A summer resident, rare in North Greenland, quite common in the southern division, breeding throughout its range
up to 69° N. lat. The earliest eggs laid on the 30th of
May, last found on the 10th of August.

[These dates suggest the possibility of two broods being
reared, though I do not remember of having seen this fact
recorded. — M. C.]

4. Red-throated Loon. (*Urinator lumme.*)

A summer resident; breeds everywhere throughout the
country; eggs found on June 10 and July 25.

5. Tufted Puffin. (*Lunda cirrhata.*)

An accidental visitor.

[It may be considered unwise to give this Pacific-coast
species a place here, unless its claim be supported by definite testimony of undoubted reliability; but it must not be
forgotten that Pastor Moschler alleged to have received
skins from Greenland, and that Audubon states that he shot
on the Kennebec River the specimen he figured. Professor
Newton omitted the name from his list of Greenland birds,
thinking Moschler made a mistake in referring his examples

to this species. The name appeared in my "Catalogue
of the Birds of New Brunswick" on the authority of Mr.
Boardman, who has lately informed me that he was mis-
taken in the identification. — M. C.]

6. Puffin. (*Fratercula arctica.*)

Breeds sparingly along the whole coast, though more frequent in the northern than in the southern division. Eggs
found on June 1 and June 10. Reinhardt states that only
one form of *Fratercula* occurs in Greenland, and he *believes*
that it is *arctica*, — the common European Puffin.

[The variety named *glacialis* by Leach has been omitted,
though this is either a Greenland bird or it is a myth, as
Leach's type came from that country. Cassin reported seeing specimens from Greenland, and Howard Saunders considers it plentiful on the coast, up to the 70th parallel.
Professor Newton found this form at Spitzbergen in company with true *arctica*. Mr. Ridgway states that the
two appear to differ only in size, *glacialis* being the
larger. — M. C.]

7. Black Guillemot. (*Cepphus grylle.*)

Resident, common, breeding everywhere. Eggs laid from
June 10 to July 25.

[NOTE. — It is probable that Mandt's Guillemot (*Cepphus
Mandtii*) occurs in Greenland. — M. C.]

8. Murre. (*Uria troile.*)

Rare; probably breeds in small numbers.

9. Brünnich's Murre. (*Uria lomvia.*)

Resident; breeds in great numbers north of 64°, and probably to the southward of that line. During winter it is

found in great numbers in South Greenland. Eggs were taken on June 15.

10. Razor-billed Auk. (*Alca torda*.)

A summer resident, not uncommon either in North Greenland or South Greenland, and breeds along the whole coast. Eggs were taken June 2 and June 30.

11. Great Auk. (*Plautus impennis*.)

Formerly occurred in Greenland, — now extinct.

12. Dovekie. (*Alle alle*.)

Breeds in North Greenland, its most southerly nesting-place being near Egedesminde in about 69° N. lat. During winter it is often very numerous in South Greenland.

13. Skua. (*Megalestris skua*.)

Occasionally seen along the shore of South Greenland.

14. Pomarine Jaeger. (*Stercorarius pomarinus*.)

A summer visitor, nesting between 64° and 73° N. lat., and is the most common Jaeger of North Greenland.

15. Parasitic Jaeger. (*Stercorarius parasiticus*.)

A summer resident, nesting quite commonly in South Greenland, even up to 69° N. lat. Eggs were taken from June 4 to July 25.

16. Long-tailed Jaeger. (*Stercorarius longicaudus*.)

Breeds somewhat rarely and only north of 62½° N. lat.

17. Ivory Gull. (*Gavia alba.*)

Not uncommon, but certainly does not breed within the settled parts of the country.

18. Kittiwake. (*Rissa tridactyla.*)

A summer resident, common all over Greenland, and breeding in great numbers, especially in the southern division. Eggs were taken on June 3 and June 18.

19. Glaucous Gull. (*Larus glaucus.*)

Very common; breeds in all suitable localities. Many remain over winter, especially young birds. Eggs were taken from May 10 to June 14.

20. Iceland Gull. (*Larus leucopterus.*)

Breeds everywhere in Greenland, but most abundantly in the southern part, where it is extremely numerous. A few, chiefly young birds, remain in South Greenland over winter. Eggs laid from May 14 to June 10.

[Note. — As Kumlien's Gull (*Larus kumlieni*) has been found breeding on Cumberland Bay, it doubtless occurs on the western coast of Greenland. — M. C.]

21. Great Black-backed Gull. (*Larus marinus.*)

A resident, common, especially along the shores of Central Greenland. Eggs laid from May 3 to June 15.

22. Siberian Gull. (*Larus affinis.*)

A chance visitor.

23. Herring Gull. (*Larus argentatus.*)

A chance visitor in South Greenland.

24. Ross's Gull. (*Rhodostethia rosea.*)

An occasional visitor.

[Mr. Howard Saunders states that only six specimens of this rarest of the Gulls are known to have been captured in Greenland. — M. C.]

25. Sabine's Gull. (*Xema sabinii.*)

Somewhat rare. Benzon obtained nine skins from various districts of Greenland, taken from latitude 64° to the most northerly settlement.

26. Common Tern. (*Sterna hirundo.*)

A summer resident, breeding in both North and South Greenland.

27. Arctic Tern. (*Sterna paradisæa.*)

[This Tern occurs in great abundance on both shores of Greenland, and has been found breeding as far north as 82° 34'. Captain Fielden reports finding a pair of young birds nearly ready for flight, early in August, in lat. 81° 50'. — M. C.]

28. Fulmar. (*Fulmarus glacialis.*)

29. Lesser Fulmar. (*Fulmarus glacialis minor.*)

Reinhardt mentions both forms of Fulmar among the birds of Greenland. Probably it is *F. glacialis* that is found chiefly off the south coast; while *F. glacialis minor* breeds in vast numbers north of the 69th parallel. This

seems to be supported by the fact that eggs collected in
North Greenland are smaller than those from Iceland, —
the former measuring 68 by 48 mm., the latter 77 by
51 mm.

[Kumlien reports finding Fulmars breeding in myriads
at Ovifak, in Greenland, and this is confirmed by other
observers. These breeding birds may, however, be of the
smaller race, as suggested by the present author. — M. C.]

30. Gray Shearwater. (*Puffinis kuhlii.*)

A occasional visitor.

[Kumlien reported finding this bird in Grinnell Bay, but
the correctness of the report was questioned, and the name
was placed on the " hypothetical list " by the A. O. U.
Committee, on the ground that no example of the species
had been taken on the Western side of the Atlantic. Its
usual habitat is south of 40°, being especially abundant
in the Mediterranean; but Professor Newton states that
Moschler received a specimen from Greenland, which is now
in the Leyden Museum. Saunders considers the species
identical with *P. borealis* of Cory. — M. C.]

31. Greater Shearwater. (*Puffinus major.*)

Numerous about the coasts of South Greenland, up to 65½°
N. lat. Probably breeds.

32. Manx Shearwater. (*Puffinus puffinus.*)

An occasional visitor. Mr. Benzon had the skin of an
albino from Umanak, 1872. (E. Fencker.)

33. Bulwer's Petrel. (*Bulweria bulweri.*)

An occasional visitor.

34. Stormy Petrel. (*Procellaria pelagica.*)

An occasional visitor.

35. Leach's Petrel. (*Oceanodroma leucorhoa.*)

Quite common along the South Greenland coast, as far north as 65° N. lat., and perhaps breeds there. It is occasionally found in Disco Bay.

36. Gannet. (*Sula bassana.*)

An occasional visitor.

37. Cormorant. (*Phalacrocorax carbo.*)

A resident, breeding along the whole coast, but most numerous in North Greenland. Eggs were found from April 28 to July 25.

38. Red-breasted Merganser. (*Merganser serrator.*)

In part a resident; breeds quite generally in both North and South Greenland. Three sets of eggs were taken on July 25.

39. Mallard. (*Anas boschas.*)

A common resident, and breeding. Eggs laid from May 26 to June 29.

40. Widgeon. (*Anas penelope.*)

An occasional visitor to South Greenland.

41. European Teal. (*Anas crecca.*)

An occasional visitor.

42. Green-winged Teal. (*Anas carolinensis.*)

An occasional visitor to South Greenland.

43. Pintail. (*Dafila acuta.*)

Rather rare.

[Perhaps "uncommon" would more accurately express the relative abundance of this species. Dr. Walker found it at Godthaab, and Professor Reinhardt met with it in both North and South Greenland. — M. C.]

44. American Scaup Duck. (*Aythya marila nearctica.*)

A rare visitor, occurring in both North and South Greenland.

45. Lesser Scaup Duck. (*Aythya affinis.*)

Very rare; may possibly breed.

46. Barrow's Golden-eye. (*Glaucionetta islandica.*)

Breeds in small numbers as far north as 69° or 70°.

47. Buffle-head. (*Charitonetta albeola.*)

A rare visitor to South Greenland.

48. Old-squaw. (*Clangula hyemalis.*)

A resident; usually breeds all along the coast; abundant during the winter in South Greenland. Eggs taken from June 1 to June 20.

49. Harlequin Duck. (*Histrionicus histrionicus.*)

A summer resident, breeding quite commonly as far north as the 69th parallel.

50. Steller's Duck. (*Eniconetta stelleri.*)

An adult male was shot in Disco Bay, North Greenland, in 1878; the skin is now in Mr. E. Fencker's collection.

51. Northern Eider. (*Somateria mollissima borealis.*)

A resident, breeding in very great numbers everywhere. Eggs were found from June 6 to July 28.

52. Pacific Eider. (*Somateria v-nigra.*)

Holboll sometimes obtained Eider Ducks of both sexes which he believed to be a cross between *S. mollissima* and *S. spectabilis.* " The bills of the females resembled those of both species." He also obtained " males of *S. mollissima,* having on the neck the lancet-shaped figure which distinguishes *S. spectabilis.*" They probably were *S. v-nigra.*

[As there is no record of this species having been taken farther to the eastward than Great Slave Lake, the insertion of the name here is open to criticism. In my opinion Holboll's supposition has more probability than Mr. Hagerup's. — M. C.]

53. King Eider. (*Somateria spectabilis.*)

Breeds sparingly between 67° and 73°; but north of 73° it is more numerous. In winter it is very common in South Greenland. Eggs laid from June 20 to July 1.

In Benzon's Catalogue there is an entry of two nests with eggs received from Julianeshaab, close to Greenland's southern extremity, but probably the names *mollissima* and *spec-. tabilis* have become interchanged.

[I think Benzon's note should not be thus discredited. We might expect to find *spectabilis* breeding at Julianeshaab, for nests have been taken much farther to the southward. — M. C.]

54. Velvet Scoter. (*Oidemia fusca.*)

A chance visitor.

55. Surf Scoter. (*Oidemia perspicillata.*)

Rare. Benzon had one skin from Julianeshaab in 1878, and in the same year one skin from Eginiarfik, in 68½° N. lat.

56. Greater Snow Goose. (*Chen hyperborea nivalis.*)

Quite rare, especially adult birds. Herr V. Müller, of Ivigtut, has informed me that in the month of June, 1884 (?), some Greenlanders near Proven (in 72° N. lat.) where he then lived, brought him a pair of adult Snow Geese just captured. These birds were later secured by Gov. E. Fencker, who added them to his collection. It seems, therefore, not improbable that this bird breeds in Greenland.

57. White-fronted Goose. (*Anser albifrons.*)

Breeds quite commonly between 66° and 72°. Eggs were found on June 7 and June 24.

58. Hutchins's Goose. (*Branta canadensis hutchinsii.*)

An occasional visitor.

59. Brant. (*Branta bernicla.*)

Common as a migratory bird along the whole coast; breeds possibly in the northern part of Danish Greenland.

60. Barnacle Goose. (*Branta leucopsis.*)

A regular autumn visitor to South Greenland.

[Reinhardt reported a rumor that had reached him of eggs of this species being taken in Greenland, but this lacks confirmation. — M. C.]

61. Whooping Swan. (*Olor cygnus.*)

Formerly nested in South Greenland, but is now only a rare visitor.

62. American Bittern. (*Botaurus lentiginosus.*)

An accidental visitor to North Greenland.

[The claim of this species to be named here rests on a report of one having been taken at Egedesminde in 1809.— M. C.]

63. European Blue Heron. (*Ardea cinerea.*)

An occasional visitor in South Greenland. In Benzon's collection there was a skin from Godthaab taken January 14, 1877.

[NOTE. — There is a record of one specimen of the Little Brown Crane (*Grus canadensis*) having been taken at Iglooik, on Baffin's Bay.— M. C.]

64. Spotted Crake. (*Porzana porzana.*)

A rare visitor in South Greenland. Benzon's collection contains a skin from Julianeshaab, dated 1878.

65. Sora. (*Porzana carolina.*)

An accidental visitor to South Greenland.

66. Corn Crake. (*Crex crex.*)

An accidental visitor to South Greenland.

67. European Coot. (*Fulica atra.*)

A chance visitor.

68. American Coot. (*Fulica americana.*)

A chance visitor.

69. Red Phalarope. (*Chrymophilus fulicarius.*)

Common, but not often seen in the breeding-season south of the 68th parallel. The eggs were found from June 3 to June 28.

70. Northern Phalarope. (*Phalaropus lobatus.*)

Breeds quite generally along the coast.

71. European Snipe. (*Gallinago gallinago.*)

Somewhat uncommon; may possibly breed.

72. Dowitcher. (*Macrorhamphus griseus.*)

An occasional visitor to South Greenland.

73. Knot. (*Tringa canutus.*)

A summer resident; most common in North Greenland, where it breeds.

74. Purple Sandpiper. (*Tringa maritima.*)

Resident; breeds everywhere along the coast. Eggs found from May 14 to July 24.

75. Pectoral Sandpiper. (*Tringa maculata.*)

A rare guest in South Greenland.

76. White-rumped Sandpiper. (*Tringa fuscicollis.*)

Not uncommon in the most southerly part of Greenland, where it probably breeds.

77. Least Sandpiper. (*Tringa minutilla.*)

An occasional visitor in North Greenland.

78. Dunlin. (*Tringa alpina.*)

Somewhat rare ; possibly breeds.

79. Curlew Sandpiper. (*Tringa ferruginea.*)

Not uncommon in North Greenland. Breeds at Christianshaab, 69°.

80. Sanderling. (*Calidris arenaria.*)

Somewhat rare ; breeds north of 68°.

81. Black-tailed Godwit. (*Limosa limosa.*)

A chance visitor to South Greenland.

82. Yellow-legs. (*Totanus flavipes.*)

An accidental visitor.

83. Solitary Sandpiper. (*Totanus solitarius.*)

A chance visitor. Benzon obtained the skin of an old bird from Kangek (64° N. lat.), taken August 1, 1878.

84. Hudsonian Curlew. (*Numenius hudsonicus.*)

An accidental visitor to South Greenland.

85. Eskimo Curlew. (*Numenius borealis.*)

An accidental visitor.

86. Whimbrel. (*Numenius phæopus.*)

An occasional visitor, and may breed.

87. Lapwing. (*Vanellus vanellus.*)

An accidental visitor.

88. Black-bellied Plover. (*Charadrius squatarola.*)

Rare. Benzon obtained a skin from Greenland in 1851.

[Holboll considered that the number of these birds was increasing in Greenland. — M. C.]

89. Golden Plover. (*Charadrius apricarius.*)

A chance visitor.

90. American Golden Plover. (*Charadrius dominicus.*)

Somewhat rare; possibly breeds.

91. Ring Plover. (*Æyialitis hiaticula.*)

Breeds along the whole coast, though rather sparsely· Eggs taken June 14.

[Kumlien reports this species "very common" about Disco Island. — M. C.]

92. Turnstone. (*Arenaria interpres.*)

Somewhat rare; breeds both in North Greenland and in South Greenland.

93. Oystercatcher. (*Hœmatopus ostralegus.*)

A chance visitor to South Greenland.

94. Reinhardt's Ptarmigan. (*Lagopus rupestris reinhardti.*)

A resident; breeds in large numbers everywhere. Eggs laid from June 10 to June 20. Number of eggs in a set, 6 to 12.

95. Gray Sea Eagle. (*Haliæetus albicilla.*)

Resident, quite common; breeds everywhere, but chiefly in South Greenland. Eggs found from April 1 to –May 17. Number of eggs in set, 1 to 3.

96. White Gyrfalcon. (*Falco islandus.*)

Breeds in North Greenland; common during winter in South Greenland.

97. Gray Gyrfalcon. (*Falco rusticolus.*)

Resident; common in South Greenland, where it breeds. The exact limits of the nesting-grounds of these two forms of Gyrfalcon cannot, however, be definitely settled, as they are considered as one and the same species. The following data applies equally to both : —

Eggs laid from April 16 to May 27. Number of eggs in a set, 3 to 4.

98. Duck Hawk. (*Falco peregrinus anatum.*)

Not uncommon; breeds in both North and South Greenland. Eggs found from April 13 to June 15.

99. Merlin. (*Falco regulus.*)

A chance visitor off the coast.

100. Kestrel. (*Falco tinnunculus.*)

A chance visitor off the coast.

101. American Osprey. (*Pandion haliaëtus carolinensis.*)

A chance visitor to North Greenland.

102. Short-eared Owl. (*Asio accipitrinus.*)

Somewhat rare; not observed north of 70°.

103. Snowy Owl. (*Nyctea nyctea.*)

Fairly common, especially in North Greenland, where a few pairs breed.

104. Yellow-bellied Sapsucker. (*Sphyrapicus varius.*)

An accidental visitor to South Greenland.

105. Flicker. (*Colaptes auratus.*)

An accidental visitor.

106. Chimney Swift. (*Chætura pelagica.*)

A chance visitor to South Greenland.

107. Olive-sided Flycatcher. (*Contopus borealis.*)

A chance visitor to South Greenland.

108. Yellow-bellied Flycatcher. (*Empidonax flaviventris.*)

One taken at sea, off Cape Farewell, September, 1878.

109. Little Flycatcher. (*Empidonax pusillus.*)

A chance visitor to South Greenland.

110. Skylark. (*Alauda arvensis.*)

A chance visitor.

111. Horned Lark. (*Otocoris alpestris.*)

A chance visitor to South Greenland.

112. Northern Raven. (*Corvus corax principalis.*)

Resident; breeds in large numbers in South Greenland; less abundant in the northern division. Eggs taken on April 11 and May 9. Number of eggs in set, 3 to 5.

113. Starling. (*Sturnus vulgaris.*)

An accidental visitor.

114. Yellow-headed Blackbird. (*Xanthocephalus xanthocephalus.*)

A chance visitor to South Greenland.

115. White-winged Crossbill. (*Loxia leucoptera.*)

Rare in South Greenland.

116. Greenland Redpoll. (*Acanthis hornemannii.*)

Resident; breeds quite commonly north of 69°. In winter it occurs farther south.

117. Greater Redpoll. (*Acanthis linaria rostrata.*)

A summer visitor, but is occasionally met with in small flocks or singly in winter. It is very prolific in South Greenland, but less so in North Greenland. Eggs laid from May 20 to June 27. Number of eggs in a set, 4 to 6.

118. Snowflake. (*Plectrophenax nivalis.*)

Very numerous; breeds throughout the country. The majority migrate, but a small number remain over winter. Eggs laid from May 25 to June 25. Number of eggs in a set, 5 to 8.

119. Lapland Longspur. (*Calcarius lapponicus.*)

A summer visitor; breeds anywhere in North Greenland, as well as in the southern division (at least as far as 70½° N. lat.). Eggs laid from June 11 to July 6. Number of eggs in a set, 5 to 8.

120. White-crowned Sparrow. (*Zonotrichia leucophrys.*)

Occurs sparingly in South Greenland; may perhaps lay eggs there.

121. Barn Swallow. (*Chelidon erythrogaster.*)

A chance visitor to South Greenland.

(NOTE. — In Mr. Benzon's Catalogue there is an entry of
a defective skin of *Hirundo rustica* ♂ from Sydproven in
60° N. lat., taken June 12, 1882.   But as there is no other
evidence that this European form has been found in Greenland, and as the identification in this instance was based
wholly upon a defective skin, I think it best not to include
the species among the birds of Greenland for the present.)

122. Red-eyed Vireo. (*Vireo olivaceus.*)

A chance visitor.

123. Nashville Warbler. (*Helminthophila ruficapilla.*)

A chance visitor in South Greenland.

124. Parula Warbler. (*Compsothlypis americana.*)

A chance visitor in South Greenland.

125. Myrtle Warbler. (*Dendroica coronata.*)

A chance visitor.

126. Black-poll Warbler. (*Dendroica striata.*)

A chance visitor to South Greenland.

127. Blackburnian Warbler. (*Dendroica blackburniæ.*)

A young bird shot at Frederickshaab, South Greenland,
probably belonged to this kind.

128. Black-throated Green Warbler. (*Dendroica virens.*)

A chance visitor to South Greenland.

129. Mourning Warbler. (*Geothlypis philadelphia.*)

A chance visitor to South Greenland.

130. Canadian Warbler. (*Sylvania canadensis.*)

A chance visitor. Mr. Benzon obtained the skin of a young bird from Greenland in 1875.

131. White Wagtail. (*Motacilla alba.*)

A chance visitor, to both North and South Greenland.

132. American Pipit. (*Anthus pensilvanicus.*)

Occurs, when migrating, in South Greenland, and breeds to some small extent north of 66°, 50' N. lat.

133. Meadow Pipit. (*Anthus pratensis.*)

A chance visitor to South Greenland.

134. Long-billed Marsh Wren. (*Cistothorus palustris.*)

A chance visitor to South Greenland.

135. Ruby-crowned Kinglet. (*Regulus calendula.*)

A chance visitor to South Greenland.

136. Gray-cheeked Thrush. (*Turdus aliciæ.*)

A chance visitor to South Greenland. Mr. Benzon obtained a skin from Greenland, taken August, 1852.

It is possible that this is the same kind as Reinhardt entered as *Turdus minor.*

137. Red-winged Thrush. (*Turdus iliacus.*)

A chance visitor to South Greenland.

138. American Robin. (*Merula migratoria.*)

A chance visitor to South Greenland.

139. Wheatear. (*Saxicola œnanthe.*)

A summer resident; breeds everywhere. Eggs laid from May 30 to June 28. Number of eggs in a set, 5 to 8.

From the above it will be seen that the birds of Greenland are drawn more from America than from Europe. About one half of the different species are merely chance visitors, and of these only a small number are found in North Greenland.

[Of the one hundred and thirty-nine species here enumerated one is extinct and fifty-three are merely accidental stragglers, while twenty-four others are so rare that they might be classed with the accidentals, leaving but sixty-one species that should be recognized as regular inhabitants of Greenland; and of these several are of quite uncommon occurrence. — M. C.]

www.ingramcontent.com/pod-product-compliance
Lightning Source LLC
Chambersburg PA
CBHW030854260626
47169CB00008B/2529